IT'S NOT WHAT YOU THINK

ANSELMA YARDE

outskirts
press

A MOTHER'S GUILT

Imet him at the stairs. I looked down at the replica of him and smiled. One was about two feet two inches shorter. One had big hands, big feet and toned muscles. But anyone looking into the light brown eyes of the smaller male, would be sure to see the same intensity and playfulness mirrored in the others eyes. I looked up and my smile faded, there would be no warmth toward s this one.

"Be sure to have him back by five." Will he ever speak to me with the love he once did? I remembered how his words use to ooze with love. I hated it so much. I didn't want such folly from him. I couldn't bear to look at him now. I had to do something to shake him up. I hated that he could be so calm. "Whatever." The word he hated most. I knew this would get to him. I hoped it would.

"I'm serious, no later than five. Bye, Mickey, later." Stay calm, how this made me simmer. But I had to be good. I had my son to think about. Remember what the therapist said; *If you can't do it for you, do it for Mickey.* I would bite my tongue and fight the urge to retaliate against my perceived threat. I can do it, I know I can. I have to go or I will surely break. Mickey waved goodbye to his father, and we turned and walked down the stairs into the street. I took a deep breath.

At last I was alone with my son. Oh how I love this child. The glare of the sun blinded me for a moment. I pulled out my sun-glasses so I could shade my eyes from the glare. I turned to Mickey and pulled his hat lower to cover his eyes. He pushed it up again. I smiled, for I had forgotten that he hated his hat low. Things needed to change soon or I would forget more things. I needed to curb these thoughts or I will lose it.

I looked down at Mickey and my heart lurched. Oh how I love this kid. I have loved him for eight years. Three of them have been spent away from him. I hated being a three hour every Saturday mom. But I yearned for these visits, for it could be worse and I could never see him again. For this my ex-husband and the whole world wanted me to feel grateful. I shifted my thoughts, for I refused to let anything impinge on my time with my son.

I told Mickey the plan for the day. First we would go to the zoo, and then maybe have something to eat. I figured he already had lunch and I would be returning him before dinner. After that I thought we could go to the playground, and pass the time until those horrid stairs. Those stairs where my heart begins to crumble into tiny fragments at the inevitable loss that occurs there. Those stairs where I let go of Mickey's hand and feel as though I am letting go of my life line. Those bus station stairs where I try hard to control my overwhelming urge to scream.

The upside to these Saturday visits was that for three hours I had Mickey all to myself. I did not have to refuse him anything. Whatever he wanted to do, wherever he wanted to go, I could make it happen. But I couldn't give him the one thing he longed for, and no matter how many times I tried to explain it to him he just didn't understand. The question he asked every Saturday, the question that haunted my dream at night. *Are you better now, can you come home?* That is the one thing I could never give him. I could never go to that place he called home again.

Mickey and I had a wonderful time at the zoo. We chatted about school and all the things I've been missing out on. He told me about his soccer team, and he wanted me to come and watch his game on Sunday. I couldn't go of course, but I wish I could, so I lied to my son. Next time I promised. Promises I could never keep, and promises that will surely haunt him as he grew up. Someday he would stop looking at me through an eight year-old's eyes, and then I wonder if I'll ever see him again.

It was now three-thirty, another thing I hated, thinking about the time. I decided to take him to the park for half an hour, and then make my way back. I watched him climb the jungle-gym as though he had really evolved from a monkey. As I watched, my memories crowded me as they did when the end was near. The pain I felt at having such little time with him swelled until I couldn't breathe. I remembered the slaps; the screams; the shoving; the crying; the loss. I thought of the rage that shook me to my core. It would overtake me and I would be helpless under its power. Oh how I wished I could go back and change those times when my rage got the better of me. But it was too late.

I remembered the blood; the bruises; the swollen hands; and the handcuffs. They were not cold like steel usually is, but they were hard and constricting. I felt like a trapped animal, and I screamed and yelled like one. In my periphery I saw that my son was watching the entire thing from the door-way of his room. My heart had sunk because this was the one thing my son had never known about me. He stood there crying and I wanted to die. In my rage I had not seen him enter the room.

I wanted to reach out to him but I couldn't, the handcuffs deterred me. But maybe that wasn't all that stopped me. I looked into those light brown eyes and I saw something I had never seen directed at me before, FEAR. For he had witnessed me being outrageously mean to the other person he loved. I had been abusive towards my husband many times over the years, but this was the first time my son had borne witness to it. My husband took him from the doorway and that was the last time I saw him for three years.

That was how long it took me to get control over the anger I carried around for all males. I learned from an early age to attack first and you would always be the one with the power. My mother taught me that every time she cowered when my father attacked her. She taught me that when she would still prepare meals for, clean for, and sleep with her abuser. If it worked for my father why shouldn't it work for me? But unlike my father I had always shielded my son from the horror that was his mother.

I shook away the memories for I was on my way to trying to deal with my anger. The only part I hated was that I could never raise my son. As much as it hurt, I knew it was the best thing for him to be raised by someone who was not prone to bouts of rage. Unlike my mother, I wanted to protect my son from an abusive parent, even if that parent was me. And for that the judge had awarded me three hour Saturday visits.

I took Mickey back to the bus station; we sat on a bench and ate ice-cream. We chatted about what we could do the next Saturday. I told him how much I loved him and I would be counting the days until I saw him again. Then I looked at the clock and moved towards the stairs. The bigger replica approached us, on time as usual, as though he thought I wouldn't return with Mickey. I hugged my son one last time and walked towards my ex-husband. I met him on the stair

IF YOU SEE SOMETHING, SAY NOTHING!

"Hello, may I please speak to a detective? I want to report a crime."

"Hold on please."

"Hello, this is Detective Synder, may I help you?"

"Yes, my name is Marcie Small. There is something shady going on next door."

"Shady? Go ahead ma'am."

"Well, my neighbor always has these guests over, but I have never seen any of them leave."

"That's not a crime, ma'am."

"But I heard a scream last-night and I just want someone to come check it out."

There was a brief pause and some muffled sounds on the detective's end. The detective told Marcie that he would send a cruiser by to check things out. After he had taken her address, he bid her good day and hung up.

After Marcie returned the receiver to its base, she went into the kitchen to brew some coffee. She looked across the yard to Mr. Kerry's backyard and frowned. His yard was very put together, and she wondered when he took care of it. She never saw him in his yard. She had wanted to go over to his house this morning and speak to him about the scream. She hadn't known how to go about it. So she had decided to let the police handle it. She hoped that they would get to the bottom of whatever was going on over there.

Marcie sat in her rocker in the living room to wait for the cops. What was taking them so long? She decided that she would give them another twenty minutes. Then she would go over and snoop – no investigate! Her rocker was positioned to see the street from the front, and Mr. Kerry's side-door at her right. She needed to make sure he didn't leave before they got here. She saw the cruiser pull up and park in front of her house. Two officers got out, one male, the other female.

She had the door opened before they reached the patio. They looked up at her and she smiled and welcomed them into her home. The male officer introduced himself as Officer Rogers, and his partner as Officer Cummings. Marcie couldn't wait to tell them all about all the strange happenings going on around the neighborhood, but they kept asking her direct questions.

"Can you tell us about the scream?"

That was the female officer, she seemed so no-nonsense. She told them about Mr. Kerry's guests who went in but never came out. She told them about her late night backyard check when she heard the scream. They exchanged glances. She was very sorry she told them about the midnight check. She didn't want them to think that she was a snoop.

"Can you describe the guests?" Detective Rogers had his pencil posed to write down her information.

"All types of people go there. Black, White, Asians and

Hispanics. Which is weird because he's not that friendly to his neighbors."

"Let's get back to the scream. Did you see anything else while you were out *checking* the yard?" Cummings asked.

"No, but I'm sure something weird is going on."

When she had told them everything, they bid her good-day. They said that they would go and check out her story. She watched them go and she sat on the porch with her knitting. After a short period, they returned their cruiser. They did not even tell her what they had found out. After she had taken the time to call, and given them so much information. Maybe they didn't ask enough questions, or they weren't taking he seriously. She decided to call the station again.

"Hello, may I please speak to Detective Rogers or Detective Cummings please; tell them it's Marcie Small."

"Hold on," the elevator music came on.

"I'm sorry, Ms Small, but the detectives are busy. Can I help you with something?"

"No, that's okay. Just tell them to give me a call when they are free. Thank you."

"You have a good day," the voice replied. Then click.

Marcie decided to take matters into her own hands. She walked slowly over to Mr. Kerry's house. She stood on the porch for a few seconds before she rung the bell. Mr. Kerry opened the door as if he had been waiting for her to ring the bell. He was an enormous man. His shirt was a little worn, and his pants had a zigzag stitiching on the knees.

"Whaddya want, Mizz Small?'

"Well I saw the cops over just now and I wanted to make sure everything was okay."

"I live here fuh five years, and yuh never came here."You send them cops, eh?'

"Did they say that?"

"No."

Mr. Kerry looked her up and down. She was a plump one, but tat was a good thing. It's good for a woman to have some flesh that you could sink your teeth into. He was starved for companionship. His other guests were so whiny he had to cut them off. He invited her in for something to drink. She accepted and entered the house. He knew she was admiring his good house-keeping. He never left anything out of order. He was meticulous.

"C'mon in de kitchen ma'am."

"Just call me Marcie."

"Marcie, sid down. Call me Tom."

"Okay Tom."

"What a good house-keeper you are."

"I like to keep de place spotless."

"Since my Lenny died, the house isn't that messy anymore."

"Yeah, the bald guy who died."

Marcie nodded. She was offended by his description of her Lenny. As she surveyed her surroundings, she couldn't help but find the irony. This man was so unkempt, but not a dust mite was visible. She realized that he was talking to her, and she missed what he had said.

"Sorry, what?"

"Oh, here's your drink."

"It sure is thick and red."

He gave her the glass of liquid. She raised the glass to her lips. He knew the moment she realized what it was. Her nose turned up a little. *Blood.* Before she has a chance to react, he pricked her with a needle. He took his butcher knife and cut her fingers off. One at a time. He showed them to her. She looked alarmed, but couldn't scream. Tears ran down her eyes. He smiled. Unexpectedly, he had very white teeth.

"Jus makin' sure yuh not goin' to holler. Don't want no more police. Made dat mistake once."

He poke her with the tip of the knife. Marcie's legs felt like rubber. She couldn't believe what was happening to her. The pain was unbearable. She could hear water boiling on the stove. She heard a plopping sound. In her periphery she saw him putting her fingers in the pot. Realization hit her like a punch in the gut. She saw the chainsaw and knew she would be seeing her Lenny soon; but would he recognize her in pieces? She closed her eyes, and blackness enveloped her.

Mr. Kerry finished cutting her up. It was a lot of work. He marveled at how much of her there was to slice up. He would have food for awhile. He sectioned the pieces and bagged them. He placed them in the freezer. He pulled out his pail. His bleach. His scrubbing brush. He got to work. Guests were so messy. But it kept him fed.

JEALOUSY

What is she doing here?

Tom invited her.

Did you know she was coming?

Well, he asked if I would mind and I said no.

And you never thought about how that would make me feel!

Aww, c'mon. Honey let's not start this ok!

Why is she here? You don't invite exes to your party.

It's Tom's party too, and he could invite who the hell he wants.

Just because your friends can't get over the breakup, doesn't mean I have to pay for it.

Deb, you're being ridiculous. Hi Cynthia.

Bye Cynthia.

That was rude!

Whatever.

You really have to stop this crap. This is really grating my nerves. Cynthia and I only try to be cordial and you know that. Why would I want to get back together with someone who cheated on me with my cousin while we were engage? I'm so over her.

You're over her, but she's not over you. Everywhere we

turn, there she is! I'm sick of it, and she has the nerve to come here.

Deb, I'm really not doing this with you right now.

Oh yes you are, or I'll cause a scene.

Will you stop this crap; and lower your voice, people are staring.

Screw them. I bet Tom invited her just to get a rise out of me. Well I'm not going to disappoint him.

Don't be like that; let's try to have a good time.

You have a good time! I'm going home!

What??

You can stay here with Cynthia or go home with me.

Are you for real? This is my party! Tom and I have worked very hard for this promotion, and we deserve to celebrate. He went to a lot of trouble setting this all up and I'm not leaving!!

So you rather stay with Cynthia? DON'T WALK AWAY FROM ME!

I'm not going to stand here and listen to you and your ranting. She is here so deal with it!

How come I always have to deal with it? It's easy for you to say that, you have never had to put up with any of my exes showing up wherever we are.

That's because they can't wait to get as far away from you as possible. C'mon you know I was kidding. Damn. You aren't going to cry are you?

If she stays I'm leaving, 'cause I'm not wanted here.

Nobody here gives a damn about my feelings!

What kind of bullshit is that?

Mine.

Do whatever the hell you want, I'm staying! I'm not going to let you spoil MY night! Your jealous outbursts are staring to put a crimp in my life and I don't need that bullshit!! Can't you get over this for one night?

But it isn't one night though, she's always around. I'm a woman and I know how women operate. She wants you back!

So what if she does? It takes two.

When a woman wants something she'll do whatever it takes to get it. She knows if she keeps showing up it will bother me and then I'll get upset. We will keep fighting 'til we finally break up and then she can make her move.

So she is smarter than you then. "Cause it's working. You're upset every time you see her. Don't you hear how ridiculous you sound? Aren't you a woman too? So won't you be immune to her shenanigans because you know beforehand what she's up to?

Are you making fun of me?!

No, but you're being an ass. Cynthia can only have me if I want her. Believe me, I DON'T! Ans right now I'm not sure I want you either.

Forget you then! I' leaving! You van stay and enjoy your party.

Be like that then! If you can't trust me, especially when I'm right in front of you, then this can't work.

It's not fair that I have to put up with her.

I came here with you. I'm in a relationship with you. I love you! So what's the problem?

Oh, so now you love me? You have never said that in the two years we've been together. But now, all of a sudden, you just spout it out. Screw you and your love! I'm going home! Give me my keys.

Girl, you really need to stop. I'm not playing anymore, stop you bullshit!

Or what?

Or you gonna make me get loud up in here. And I'm gonna have to strip off all my clothes and swing on the chandelier and show everybody how freaky I can get.

You so stupid.

And that's why you l-l-l-love me.

Whatever.

Come here and give me a kiss so Cynthia can see her plan ain't working. Come kiss these luscious lips.

I'm still mad. Ok, that's enough, she's not even looking.

How you know? You had your eyes open? Girl, you're too much. Let's go dance.

If she comes near us again tonight, I'm going to kick her ass up and down this place.

Umm, you know she's a black belt right? So you gonna be on your own. PARTY!!

LOVE HURTS

Saige sat at the table and waited. He took in the scenery. He hadn't been to this bar before, so everything was new to him. He liked the way the place was decorated; it wasn't overdone. The colors were all soft: pink, white, and pale blue. He wondered if a woman decorated the place.

"Would you like to order?" the waitress smiled.

"No thanks," he smiled back.

As the waitress walked away, Lyn walked in. She wore a pair of khaki slacks, and a white shirt. She usually wore jeans and T-shirts. She looked very nice. The news must be good if she was all dressed up.

"Hi, have a seat, Lyn. You look very nice."

"Thanks."

"Do you want anything to drink or eat?"

"Yes, could I have a club soda, please?"

He waved to the waitress. She took their order and returned to the bar. No-one spoke until the drinks arrived. Lyn took a sip of the club soda. Saige just stirred the ice in his. Lyn picked up one of the napkins and pinched off the edges. She had taken her time getting here. She had stood outside watching Saige for about fifteen minutes before she decided to come in. What she had to say was going to destroy him, but there was no other way.

"I think we should just get to the point," she said.

"Okay." he looked into her eyes.

"My mom wants me to come home. She thinks that our living together isn't right. I agree with her."

"What do you mean you agree? We have been living together for six months. How come your mother – who has never visited – thinks it's wrong all of a sudden?"

"Well, the reason she never visited was because she didn't approve."

"So now she has decided that you should know this?"

"Well, I told her about you asking me to marry you, and she just voiced her opinion."

"She should be happy we're doing the right thing. Are you sure this is the reason why you want to go home?"

She couldn't meet his eyes. If she allowed him to see her eyes, he would know she was lying. He had been her friend for two years. They were lovers for six months. He knew her very well. Or so he thought.

"Look, Saige, I'm not being totally honest here. There's something you need to know."

"You can tell me anything. I love you, and whatever it is we can handle it, together."

"I don't think you're going to feel the same way after I tell you."

"Trust me, there's nothing you can say to change my feelings for you."

Lyn need to get this off her chest. This was going to change his life forever. She hated what she had to do, but it had to be done. She couldn't keep lying to him.

"Lyn, stop beating around the bush. Please say what you have to say."

"As I said before, I haven't bee totally honest. First of all, my mother doesn't speak to me. We haven't spoken in six months. She put me out, and that was why I suggested that we move in together," she paused.

"What happened? Why would she be that upset with you?" he asked.

"I -uh – um -I slept with her boyfriend." She waited for his reaction. His eyes widened, his mouth dropped.

"I'm so sorry. I know we've known each other a long time, and we built our relationship on trust. I know this is going to affect our relationship. Both our love life, and our friend-ship," She took a deep breath.

He closed his eyes. He took a deep breath. "Go on."

"When we were just starting to date, I was still unsure of where it would go. Joe and I had been having these feelings, but we had not really acted on them. We made sure not to put ourselves in situations that could get us in trouble. But one day I came home from work and he was there. My mother had called to say that she was going to be late."

"Why didn't you leave?"

"He had prepared dinner, and he asked me if I wanted to eat with him since mom was going to be late. It started off in-nocent enough. We drank some wine, too much. I know that's no excuse, but it didn't help."

"So did you tell her? Did he?"

"No, she caught us in bed together. We fell asleep after because we drank too much."

"I want to be mad, but this happened before we got serious. We're together now, and that is in the past. Now that I know the truth, we can move forward. We can move past this. Right?"

Lyn did not meet his gaze. She stared at the napkin in her hand. Saige was silent. He waited. The look on her face told him there was something else. He wanted to know what she was thinking. He took her hand. She didn't pulled away as he had expected. She covered his hand with hers. She began to cry silently.

"Honey, it's okay. I forgive you." He tried to lift her chin so he could see her eyes, but she wouldn't raise her head. She continued to stare at their hands. Then she let go of his hand, and met his gaze.

"No," she whispered.

"No, what?"

"No, we can't move past this. Joe and my mom couldn't make it work. He was too young for her anyway. He called me about a month ago, and we met for drinks. We've been seeing each other since then."

"I can't believe this. How could you do this to me? Did you ever want to be with me?"

"Of course, I did. But I can't shake the feelings I have for him."

"Oh, so you are into cheaters then? Well, then I'm definitely not the guy for you."

"I'm so sorry. I didn't have to tell you about this. I could have just moved on with Joe."

'"Well, my heart thanks you for thinking of it, and trying not to totally destroy it."

"Saige, I'm really sorry. I know you're hurt, but you'll get over it.."

"You make me sick! How could you do this to me. You slut! I hope you get everything you deserve and then some."

Saige got up and stomped out of the bar. He needed to get away to clear his head. Lyn sat for a few more minutes. She paid for the drinks, and gathered her things to go. As she turned toward the door, he eyes locked onto a familiar face. Joe was staring back at her. She smiled at him, he didn't smile back. Then she saw why. She was taller then Lyn, and very curvy. The woman walked up to Joe and kissed him. He didn't fight her off. There was a familiarity to the way he held this woman at the waist. The woman snaked her arms around his neck and the kiss deepened.

Lyn felt trapped. She couldn't walk past them. She had to wait until they moved. *What had she done?*

THE BEGINNING
AND THE END

The phone rang, and he picked it up before the second ring. He had been waiting all day. He tried to collect himself before answering.

"Hello."

The calm in which he answered was in contrast to the feelings that churned within the depths of his being. He listened to the voice on the other end. He didn't recognize the voice. However, the voice related the news he waited for all day. He hung up as soon as he received the news. He gathered all of his things. His keys, notebook and briefcase. He headed towards the elevator, and rode it to the garage. He didn't have to search for his car. It was parked in his usual spot, directly ahead of the elevator.

The car was his pride and joy. It was a dark green BMW, and it was worth every penny. He took great care of it. He never parked it outside the house. He was afraid it would get stolen. He was careful to park it in the line of sight from the elevator, because there were no parking spots on either side of his car. He had lucked out getting this spot. He made sure to be at work by seven a.m. To secure that spot. He disarmed the alarm.

He walked directly to the driver's side, and unlocked the door via the remote. Unlike other days, he didn't stop to check for any imperfections that may have occurred while he was upstairs. He opened the door and climbed into the driver's seat as quickly as he could. He threw his briefcase and notebook toward the backseat. He did not check to see if they landed on the target. Any other day he would have placed them on the seat before getting into the car.

He inserted the key and started the car. He checked the review mirror. He wasn't sure why. He backed out of the parking space. As he entered the street outside the garage, his mind wandered to the news he had just received. He couldn't believe it had happened so quickly. His wife had told him not to worry. She said that it was a long process, and that he would probably reach home before it was time. She had been wrong.

He took his time; he didn't want to cause an accident. He drove as fast as the speed limit allowed. His mind went back to his news. A newborn son. He wondered whom he resembled. Did he have a button nose like his wife's? Or did he have a flared nose like his? Were his eyes hazel or dark brown? How much did he weigh? He was sorry that he missed the actual event. He had been looking forward to this day for 41 weeks.

He was so happy. He couldn't wait to see his son. He became more and more anxious. This was a short trip; why was it taking so long? He didn't realize that he had applied pressure to the accelerator. The car shot forward; it took him by surprise. Unfortunately, there was traffic entering the intersection. He had missed the STOP sign. He braced himself as he felt the bang of the collision with the other car. His car spun to the right. He tried to gain control.

The car ran off the road. Brake! Brake! His mind screamed. He reacted too quickly and lost control. The car spun around, and slammed into a tree. The front of the car was smashed. The dashboard sat in his lap. His head was pinned to the steering wheel.

A flash of memories flowed through his head. The day he went to college with his mom and dad hovering. The day he met his wife. Their wedding day. Was it only a year ago he got the job he always dreamed of? He could plainly see the smile he wore at the new of his son's conception. He recalled the nervousness he felt all day as he waited for his wife to call if she went into labor. The flashbacks continued to flow. Pictures in his mind's eye of things he had so long forgotten.

He closed his eyes as the tears ran down his cheeks. He could hear a voice asking if he was okay. He couldn't answer. He would never see his son. His son would know him through a barrage of photos. The tears continued to flow. I love you, welcome to the world. That was his last conscious thought. Five minutes away, his wife and son waited for daddy's arrival.